ANOTHER MONSTER AT THE END OF THIS BOOK

Written by Jon Stone
Illustrated by Michael Smollin

A GOLDEN BOOK • NEW YORK

 Published in the United States by Golden Books, an imprint of Random House Children's Books, a division of Random House, Inc., 1745 Broadway, New York, NY 10019, and in Canada by Random House of Canada Limited, Toronto, in conjunction with Sesame Workshop. Originally published by Golden Books Publishing Company, Inc., in conjunction with Children's Television Workshop, in 1996. Golden Books, A Golden Book, A Little Golden Book, the G colophon, and the distinctive gold spine are registered trademarks of Random House, Inc.
www.randomhouse.com/kids
www.sesameworkshop.org
Educators and librarians, for a variety of teaching tools, visit us at www.randomhouse.com/teachers
ISBN: 978-0-307-98769-3
Library of Congress Control Number: 2008935607
Printed in the United States of America
30 29 28 27 26

ELMO,
I AM NOT
GOING TO THE
END OF THIS BOOK
IF THERE IS A
MONSTER THERE!
MONSTERS are not to be
trifled with. I am
going to stay right
here on the first page.

OK, Mister Grover. ELMO will go see the monster all by himself.
TURN THE PAGE, PLEASE.

WILL YOU PLEASE STOP TURNING PAGES! Every time you turn a page we get closer to The MONSTER at the End of This Book. ELMO, come with me. We are going home NOW!
ELMO?
ELMO?
Where are you?

TURN THE PAGE.

ELMO, do you not understand that at The End of This Book there is a MONSTER?
It could be a nice, furry Monster like you or me or Cookie or Herry.
But it could also be a very BIG, SCARY, HUNGRY MONSTER with sharp teeth and claws and an ATTITUDE!

THEREFORE, I am putting these hundreds of paper clips here just to remind you that we are not going to the end of this book!
YES, Mister Grover.
TURN THE PAGE, PLEASE.

ALL RIGHT! NO MORE Mister Nice Guy!
I have now taken all your alphabet blocks and built a huge CASTLE right here! NO ONE can turn this page NOW!

TURNY, TURNY, TURN, TURN...

ENOUGH is ENOUGH!
I, Grover, am now GLUING this page down so you CANNOT turn it.
And if you cannot turn the page we will not get to The MONSTER that is at The End of This Book!

DO IT.
GLUE

ELMO, PLEASE, PLEASE
forget about seeing
The MONSTER at The End
of This BOOK
and come back with me
to the beginning of the book.
PLEASE, PRETTY PLEASE.
Little Elmo wants to see the MONSTER.
TURN THE PAGE.

THIS WILL STOP YOU FROM TURNING PAGES! I, Grover, have put up a THICK, STEEL WALL so no one can ever EVER turn this page.

WHAT DO YOU SAY TO THAT, LITTLE ELMO?
ELMO?
ELMO?
WHERE are you, ELMO?
ELMO is on the next page.

All right. We will go see the Monster.
But just one little peek.
When I say 'TURN THE PAGE,' you jump in from the back of the book and I will jump in from the front.
We will see The MONSTER and then we will run like bunny rabbits!

Listen carefully.
You tiptoe around to
the back of the book...
I, Grover, will stay here.

ARE YOU AT THE BACK of THE BOOK, Little ELMO?
Then, here we go!
ONE... TWO...
Get ready to turn the page and then run like a bunny rabbit...
THREE!!!

YES, Mister Grover.
TURN THE PAGE!

EEEE!!

I never thought that The Monster at The End of this Book would be YOU, LITTLE ELMO.
YOU
YOU
YOU
YOU
YOU
YOU
YOU
YOU
YOU
YOU
YOU
WHATEVER.

No, no, Mister Grover, YOU are The Monster at The End of This Book. I SAW YOU!
YOU
YOU
YOU
YOU
YOU
YOU
YOU
YOU
YOU
YOU
YOU

Where are you going?
Elmo is going back two pages to see The Monster again.